BRICK

FREEDOM IN THE CAGE

BOOK III

DAKIARA

COPYRIGHT

Additional copies of this book and others are available by mail.

Mind Flow Publishing & Production LLC

PO Box 48768 Cumberland, North Carolina 28331-8768

by visiting the website listed below.

Check the website for pricing.

www.mindflowpublishingproduction.com

Formatting and Cover Design by Haelah Rice Covers

Mind Flow Publishing & Production LLC

ISBN PAPERBACK 978-1-951271-22-0

ISBN EBOOK 978-1-951271-21-3

1

First Edition

DEDICATED TO MY LOVES

DaQuan, D'eja, D'ante, Kevonn and Kiara

RIP

DaQuan Jamique '95

&

Kiara Denise '00

AND TO SOME WHO HAVE GONE BEFORE ME

Mary Merriman

Burt Merriman Sr.

Naomi Thompson

Joseph H.L. Thompson

Barbara H. Whitlock

SPECIAL THANKS

To God for giving me the strength and the words to do this project.

I am blessed by the experiences to draw from. It has not always been easy.

With each project we complete, we are that much closer to touching the world. Thank you for allowing me to live my dream.

"A slow blade penetrates the shield."

No matter how long, how hard the journey, never give up... slow and steady.

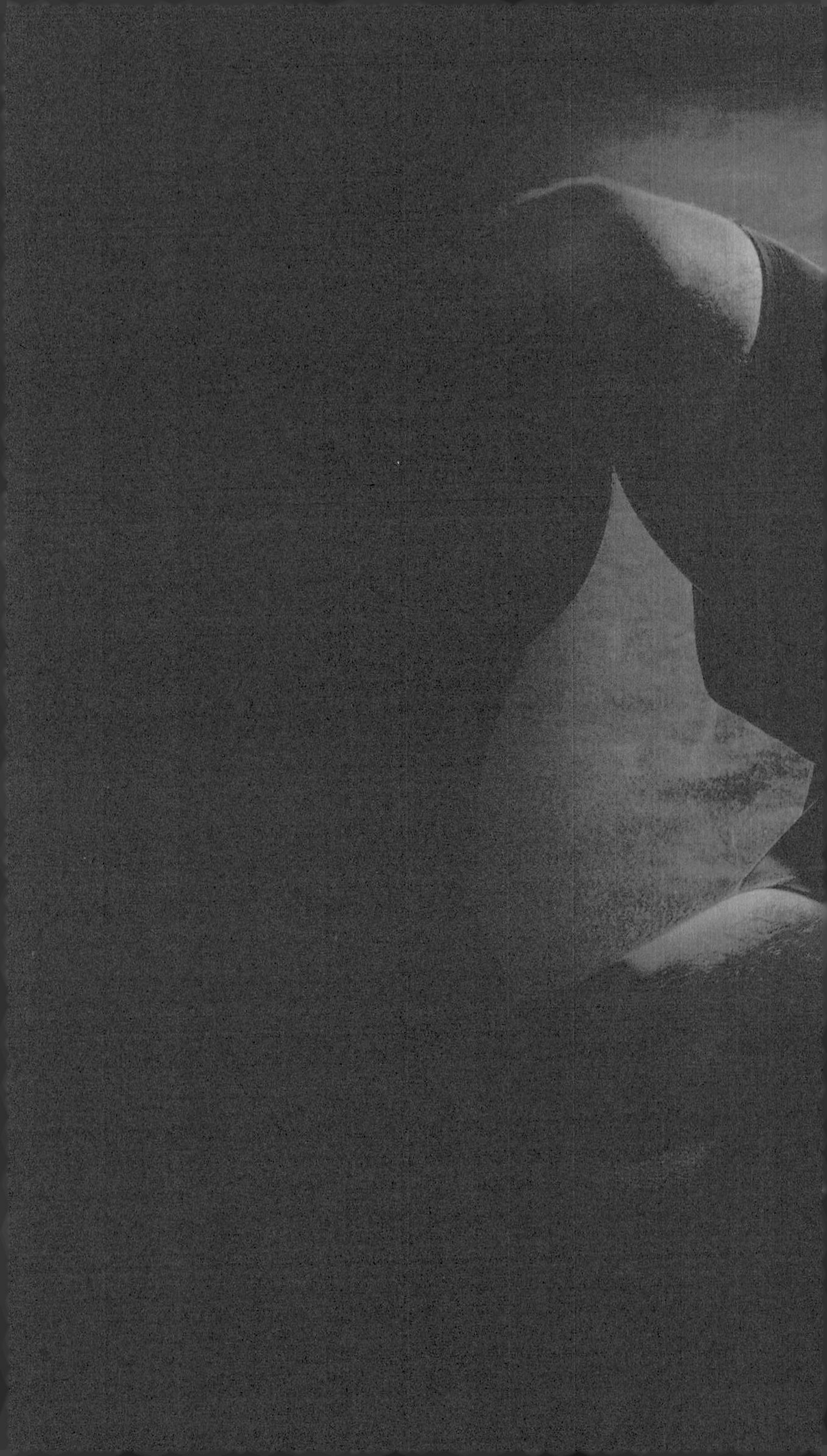

Chapter One

BRICK

Brick and Stone were working out with the punching bag early one morning. Stone noticed that it seems like Brick is working extra hard. The bag is taking a beating, and it does not appear that Brick will be letting up anytime soon. After this went on for a few more minutes, Stone had to ask Brick if something was bothering him. He groaned when one of the punches connected to the bag.

"Ouch."

He waited for a response or some type of acknowledgment from Brick, but he received none. So, he does it again on the next punch.

"Ouch, man. What in the world did I do to you?"

Brick grabbed hold of the bag so it wouldn't move. He needed a resting place. He was exerting more energy than he intended, but he needed to release some pent-up frustration.

"You know, I can tell when something is going on with one of my guys. We may not act all mushy, but I know my brothers. You can either tell me, or we just sit here all day," Stone said to his oldest friend. Whatever was going on, he could see it, and he didn't like it.

"It's nothing man. Can we just leave it alone? In these last 8 years that I have known you, we have never been mushy except for that one time after the fight."

Life drained from their faces as they remembered that day so vividly. The fight went well for Brick until his opponent got the upper hand by taking him down to the ground. Instead of just locking in and holding tight until he got the submission, he started beating on his head and wouldn't let up until the ref and trainer pulled him off. That night Brick suffered cerebral cortex damage and had to be carted out of the cage by the emergency medical team.

"Hey man," Stone punched Brick in the arm to get his attention. "Come back, man, you zoned out on me. What's got you in a tizzy this morning?"

"It's nothing, man. Well, that is not altogether true," Brick takes a long breath before he continues. "I'm worried about Shae, man. I think she is unhappy." Brick pauses before going on. "We've been getting into it over the least little things. I mean stupid things when you think about it."

Stone suggests they get away from the gym and go grab a bite so they can talk freely without prying ears. Besides, he was hungry. Which was nothing new. He was always hungry. Brick agreed, and they went to an Italian place a few blocks from the gym. They had decided it would do them good to walk it out, but their breathing was labored by the time they arrived.

"Guess we need to add more running to our routines," Stone suggested with a wry chuckle as he pulled open the door to the restaurant.

"Maybe for yourself," Brick countered. "You know you are getting old." Both men laughed. They were seated right away as they walked into Pierre's.

The hostess, Sienna, recognized them right away.

"Hey Stone, how are you doing?" She said, smiling. "It's been a minute."

Stone smiled, and his cheeks-tinged red. Brick had never seen his friend blush or be bashful around a woman before. *There is a first time for everything*. He chuckled to himself. Stone caught him snickering and punched him in the arm.

"What? Stone and Sienna sitting in the tree. K-i-s-s-i-n-g" was all he managed to get out before he was popped again. "Alright, alright, man, geez. I'm just saying you'd make a cute couple."

They were seated for only a few moments when Sienna returned with some water and to take their order. Stone tried his best to not make eye contact, but Sienna was determined to be in his sight line.

"Stone, you never smile much. I bet if we went out on a date, you would."

Again, Stone blushed and even turned his head away so she couldn't see his cheeks. He knew he would never live this down with Brick.

"You just might be right, Sienna. Who knows, maybe one day I'll get the courage to ask you out?" Before he could finish his whole sentence, she had her number written on a napkin and slid it on the table in front of him. Stone nodded and accepted it, saying he would be in touch. Feeling accomplished, Sienna walked away with a smile on her face.

Stone looked over and saw Brick smirking. Stone could only shake his head. Sienna was gorgeous. That wasn't the problem. Stone was just not in the market for companionship at the moment. His focus was rebranding and rebuilding his gym.

"Alright, man, what gives? What is going on with you and Shae?"

"Shae tripped out on me over a stupid cup being left in the sink. Not even a whole day, man. I'm not used to that. Then the other night, she came home from work and went straight to shower and then to bed without saying as many as two words to me. I tried to talk to her, and she ignored me. You know I love that woman, man, and she has been down with me since before I got hurt, but what if she is fed up? What if she is being entertained by the next dude? She is doing all kinds of interviews these days, especially with that new kid, 'The Punisher'."

"Bro, calm down, man. I know Shae, and I know she loves you more than life itself. Remember, I was there when she saw you damn near break. She was right by your side every step of the way. If there was ever a reason to leave, it would have been then, when nobody was sure you would make it. I have to admit even I had some doubts, but I am so glad you set me straight pretty quickly," Stone tried to be optimistic about Brick's situation, but he knew if he was concerned, then Shae was indeed acting out of character.

"You don't get it, man. She brought up the whole having a kid thing. I think she still blames me for her having the miscarriage when I was in the hospital, and she was stressing more than she should have been. Man, I didn't even know she was pregnant. And now she knows I cannot give her another. I finally told her this morning, I went and got tested. I needed to know if it was me, and the doctor told me my guys were all duds now. It seems as if the things helping to get my life back under control took my chances of creating life. You see, when they put you on those meds for PTSD, they neglect to tell you that your soldiers may not march the same. The meds have been causing me to drop my levels of testosterone, and that isn't good. The doc said he thought my overall wellbeing was more important. Go figure. So now this is where we are."

This caught Stone by surprise. He wanted to be there for Brick, but he was beginning to suspect he did not know how. He did know this was not the place for him, especially now. Brick should be home or wherever Shae is working on their marriage. Stone did not have any kids of his own, so he did not understand the overwhelming desire to want what one couldn't have.

"Bro, you know I don't have any children of my own. I'm more of the cool uncle type. I can say when you were down, and Shae lost the baby, it nearly broke her, but she is a fighter. She knew she had to stay strong for you. I saw her go through the grief when she was not with you. She got used to being strong and hiding her true pain. I think you need to be with her instead of at the gym. Even if you can't give her another baby, maybe look at other options. I mean, I know it won't be the same as your own blood, but you would be a hell of a dad."

"You don't get it, man, this plus her interviewing all these "new hotshots," what if one of them can offer her something I can't?" Brick dropped his head in his hands. He was all but defeated.

"Go home, bro. Remind her of why you two have made it together this long. Remind her why she is the only one for you and you for her. Fight for her. Don't give another man a chance to show her how great she is," Stone offered up some sage words of advice to his friend.

"Thanks, man. I just needed to talk it out with someone. I know I love her, and deep down, I guess I know she still loves me. I think my depression is getting the best of me. I'm going to show her we were meant for each other. That there is still a lot of our story left to tell."

That is the spirit, Stone thought. He knew those two were made for each other. Stone had seen them in love, argue like cats and dogs, and put it all back together again. They would get through this. They had to, right? That is how real love worked.

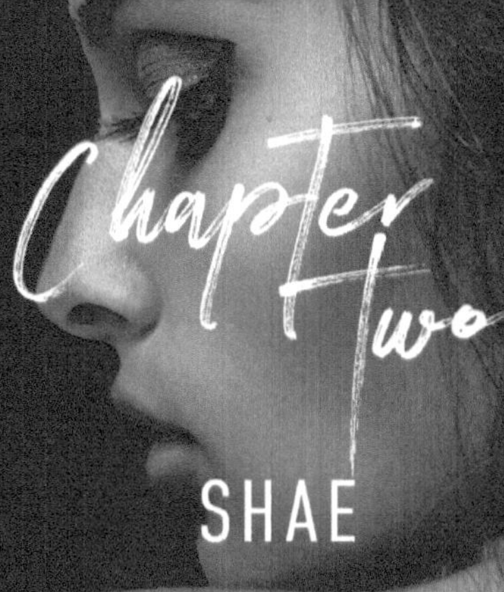

Chapter Two

SHAE

Shae is a beautiful, talented journalist who just happens to be married to Brick. She and Brick have been through some highs and some lows over the last few years, but Lord knows she loves that man. Shae has been with him to the brink of death and helped to nurse him back. All without a single thank you. But that is what you do when you love someone, right?

Shae and Brick met about ten years ago when she interviewed him as an up-and-coming sports phenom. Brick had just returned from overseas from a major kickboxing tournament, and Shae was right there. Her magazine got wind that a hometown guy was doing big things, and they loved to spotlight them.

The interviews started out well, but during them,

she got a peek into who Brick really was as a person, and that is the person she began to fall in love with. Her boss, Cassandra, had warned her against becoming personally involved with a story. Even threatened her job if she pursued him while covering his rise to fame. She didn't want the bad press to intervene with the actual authenticity of the story. Shae agreed, and as the feelings between her and Brick started growing, they agreed to chill until after she was through covering him.

The pieces she did on him turned out amazing, so much so that she won several awards, and some even garnered national attention. The day after Shae turned in the final piece, she and Brick went on their first official date. From that moment on, the two have been inseparable.

I think he sometimes takes me for granted. He doesn't appreciate the fact that I have always been right here by his side, no matter what. I don't even tell him about all the guys I could be entertaining, but I choose not to because of my love. I know he has a temper and is a bit jealous, so I try not to encourage anyone in that way.

Shae reflected upon one of their first few dates when they decided to go to Six Flags, and this young kid started eyeing Shae a little too hard.

The day was hot as it was in July, shortly after the long

Fourth of July weekend, and the place was packed. So, the pair was already slightly annoyed, or at least Brick was. He was always impatient. As they walked over to the concession booth, the kid made his way towards them. He bumped into Shae, making her drop her bag. When he bent down to pick it up, he also handed her his number. Brick, who was standing right there, witnessed the whole thing. Shae reached for his hand to make sure he kept calm. It worked until the kid smirked as he was turning to walk away. Before Shae could react, Brick dropped her hand and jumped on the kid. The kid turned around as Brick grabbed his shoulder.

"Hey man, what is your problem? I know you saw my girl and me standing there together. Are you wanting to cause a problem?"

"Dude, calm down. I'm just having fun. Besides, she didn't have to take it."

Shae remembers that part most of all because the rest of the trip had a bit of tension between her and Brick, but she promised herself that was one thing she would try to avoid. She did not like knowing Brick didn't trust her enough to know she would never step out on him. It wasn't fair that she was still paying the price for what that lame Jessica had done to him. Because of her infidelities and random hookups. Things she said Brick caused by being too busy for her. Now she must deal with this.

That was ten years ago, and now here they were,

happily married. At least most days, they were. Over the past year, Shae had felt like something was missing, but she could not put her finger on it. She had brought up to him that she was ready to have a child. When she was pregnant and lost their baby boy, she shouldered most of that alone, with some help from Stone. Brick didn't even know she was pregnant until it was over. Shae did not know that Brick had gone and gotten tested to find out what was going on until this morning. She resented the way he threw it out there, like it was just some random conversation. She had no idea just how much he was hurting. Truthfully, she was not sure she cared. Shae was being selfish, and she knew it, but a part of her needed to be that way. Maybe her husband would notice her again before it was too late.

After their heated discussion, Shae headed off to work. She hated going in when they have argued. It almost always ruined her entire day. Today would be no different. She had tried to get mentally prepared for her interview that would be coming up in the next few days with 'The Punisher'. Shae would be spending the bulk of those days with him, getting to know him and his habits to help her develop her peace. When it came to her interviews, it wasn't just a meetup and start asking questions. She liked to get to know the interviewee so that her viewers would be able to identify with them. It usually always made the pieces better.

In doing her homework, she found out that The Punisher, whose actual name was Eugene Mecari, was a guy from humble beginnings and projects. In her mind, she pictured the questions she would ask, and hopefully, he would maybe let her get footage of his family home.

The Punisher was very attractive for a fighter, not to say that all fighters looked horrible, just the opposite, in fact. Shae had always been attracted to the bad boy looks, but just not the attitude.

She was thankful for this assignment. Needing the change of atmosphere to keep her mind clear of what was going on with her and Brick. They had disagreements before or differences of opinions, but this seemed to be hanging over them like a noxious cloud, and she could not just let it go. She loved Brick. There was no question about that, but a part of her just wanted him to feel her pain and understand that she lost something she would never have again if they were together.

Shae was deep into her feelings until Eugene, The Punisher, walked in with a few bodyguards and members of his entourage. Shae could feel her knees go a little weak when their eyes connected for only a brief second. *Get your mind right Shae, you are a married woman. I know, but he is so handsome.* She had been following him for a bit now, and she liked how he carried himself. He wasn't cocky or arrogant like others she had seen. She loved how he never let his beginnings dictate how he moved through life.

She made her adjustments to her mindset, and by the time he reached out his hand to her, she was composed and back on her professional level.

"Hi Punisher, my name is Shae Brickson, and I will have the pleasure of interviewing you," she said as she shook his hand briskly. As Shae was releasing his hand and pulling hers away, she felt a gentle tug on her fingers. She looked up only to see Eugene with a wide smile that showed off his two gold teeth. Shae quickly dropped his hand as she flashed a smile of her own. Although she and Brick were in the middle of whatever this was, she could not bring herself to entertain this guy or any other. It did feel good to be acknowledged as a woman, though, even if it was only for a moment.

"Mr. Punisher, it seems you and I will be spending a few days together. I hope you are okay with that."

He nodded his head in agreement and flashed those straight pearly whites with just the accents of gold on the two bottom fangs. Clearly, Eugene was thinking he was going to enjoy this time more than

Shae. She could admit to herself that she was flirting with that line.

Shae showed him to her office, where they sat down. Punisher dismissed everyone except his publicist/manager. He joked with his guys that he felt safe.

"There is a brunch bar in the conference room two doors down on the left. You can't miss it."

Punisher instructed his bodyguards to bring his water back when they finished. Troy, who was his number one, gave Punisher the thumbs up, and within seconds he and his guys were gone.

"Well, now, Mr. Punisher, or shall I call you Eugene for this interview?" Shae inquired.

Hearing his legal name still caught Punisher off guard at times. He had garnered the moniker 'The Punisher' when he was a kid on the wrestling and football teams in school. When he played football, he did his job well. His whole high school career, he left each football game with no less than four sacks. The quarterbacks hated to play against him. This kid was relentless, and the only name that fit him was 'The Punisher', so it eventually stuck.

"Not sure who let that name get out, but since you already have it, I guess Eugene is fine." Looking over at his manager/publicist, he murmured, "remind me to get that name erased from my Wikipedia."

"Sure thing, boss man."

Shae pulled out her notepad and tape recorder, as well as her consent paperwork. She always liked to reassure her interviewees that she had the best intentions and would only print what they were comfortable with. In her career, she only had one who was not comfortable being recorded due to being set up with an audio recording when he was younger.

Shae asked several questions that he answered freely. When she got to the personal ones, she saw that he was more reserved with answering.

"When did you know this is what you wanted to do? That you wanted to fight your way through life, so to speak?" Shae inquired.

"I just knew it was something I was good at. I wanted something better for my family than our humble beginnings. I knew I could be more than the product of my environment."

"Could you explain a little more if you don't mind?" Shae quizzed.

"You know, the stereotypical one-parent family, but it wasn't because one left or was a deadbeat. My mom died from breast cancer." Shae saw his face begin to stiffen at the memory. "I lost my mom when I was seven, and my pops had to step in and step-up big time. In the blink of an eye, he was forced to be a provider and nurturer to three young boys. I was determined to make something of myself, even more so when my youngest brother Philip was killed by a stray bullet meant for someone else. Unfortunately, the bullet meant for me was taken by my brother, and he didn't stand a chance."

Punisher put his head down and rubbed his temples with his thumbs. It seemed to calm him down. His breathing had become jagged, but it was returning to normal slowly. As he was about to continue, Shae stopped him. Most reporters would have pushed ahead, but she is good conscious, could not. She would not open this man or anyone up to be that vulnerable.

"It's okay Punisher, I deeply apologize for touching upon an emotional time in your life. We do not have to use any of that. We can figure something else out to talk about."

"I am a product of my people. I have no secrets from my fans. There is nothing they can do to hurt me. This is my life, and it is what made me who I am. We are good, Ma, I promise."

He seemed a bit more at ease as the conversation progressed. Punisher even had a few anecdotes that he shared with her.

This interview phase lasted about an hour and a half. Once both parties were satisfied with the content, they decided to call it a night.

As Shae was standing to leave, Punisher rushed

over to pull her chair out for her. After thanking him, Shae started walking towards the door, hoping that he would follow.

"What time would be good for us to get started tomorrow? The earlier, the better. We can get in and out before all your fans find out you are there."

They agreed on meeting at 9 am and figured that they should be done by 11 am. That way, they would have time to get the piece nailed down and enjoy the rest of their day. Punisher had some promotion he needed to get done. Shae just wanted to get back home so she could rest.

Punisher thanked her for the time and the interview and leaned in for a hug, as he was saying how much he looked forward to seeing her tomorrow. As Shae pulled away, she could feel Punisher tightening up his hold. He bent down to whisper in her ear, "I know you want me. I can always tell."

Shae pushed him back and shook her head. She did not want to jeopardize the gig, but she did not want him getting too comfortable, either. She chatted with her boss before she left for the day. Maybe she could come along tomorrow, she thought.

Punisher left without uttering another word.

Shae left out shortly behind him and began her search for Cassandra. She found her in her office on a phone call with Punisher, no less. From what she could hear, he told Cassandra he thought things were going well so far, and he was looking forward to tomorrow. He thanked her for pairing him up with a professional such as Shae. Cassandra thanked him and hung up the phone and turned her attention to Shae.

"Well, Shae, my dear, you have wowed again. You are constantly knocking it out of the park with these interviews. I am glad that I gave you this assignment. We might even get an exclusive after the fight. Wouldn't that be awesome? But anyway, what's on your mind?"

Shae decided not to ruin her boss's moment with her insecurities. She decided she would put on her big girl panties and get it done without incident.

"Oh, nothing. I just wanted to let you know it was a good sit-down. Tomorrow, we go to where he grew up, and then we will do a final Q & A session. I should have it edited and wrapped up in the next few days."

"Outstanding!" Cassandra called out as she turned in her chair to get back to her computer. Just as Shae was about to exit the door, she spoke over her shoulder, "Don't mess this up." Shae closed the door behind her as she headed to her office to grab her bag so she could call it a night. Shae tried to call Brick to see if he needed her to pick up anything on her way home. He did not answer. Shae thought he might be asleep. Sure enough, when she got home, he was knocked out on the couch. She tiptoed through the house so as not to wake him. She was not in the mood for a serious discussion or to continue their argument from earlier. Shae took her shower and make it to bed without disturbing him. A few hours later, she felt him climb into bed.

Chapter Three

BRICK

Brick did not even hear Shae come home last night, but as he looked over at her sleeping so peacefully and he yearned to tell her everything that was in his heart. He loved this woman more than life itself, and he was afraid, probably for one of the first times in his life. Brick was terrified that she would leave him, and he would have no one to blame but himself. As he got up off the bed, he walked around and gave her a kiss on her forehead. She stirred just a little bit. His intent was not to wake her up, but just to let her know he was there and that he loved her. Brick then went off to make quick work of taking his shower to get to the gym. He hated getting there so early, and there was not a soul around, but then he also welcomed the solitude so he could put in work.

When he arrived at the gym, he noticed that the lights were already on and knew it could only be one person at this time of morning. He was correct. Stone had managed to beat him in yet again.

"What's up, Brother? You're here awfully early," Brick teased Stone.

The look on Stone's face was not one of amusement, however. It took a moment before he even looked directly at Brick. When he gathered his thoughts, he let out a heavy sigh.

"Hey, what's going on, Brother?" Without waiting for a response, Stone continued. "I have something to talk to you about, and I'm not even sure if I should. But if I do not, you will hear it from somewhere else, and I would hate that."

Brick's mind immediately drifted to Shae. His heart began to race, and he felt weak, as if he were going to faint. Stone observed that the color had disappeared from his cheeks, and he began to sway a bit. Stone reaches for him right before his legs gave way and manages to get Brick to a seat. Once he was steady, Stone moved to get him a cup of water from the water cooler on the other side of the room.

As he walked back to Brick, he began to talk.

"Aye, Brother, you, okay? What was that about?"

"Man, if you're about to tell me something about Shae, don't. I ain't trying to hear it. I won't hear it."

"Whoa, man, I was not even thinking about what you are going through and how I started that conversation might sound. I apologize. It has nothing to do with Shae, well, not directly. It is all about you and a decision you will have to make," Stone's heart went out to his friend. He was happy when the color started returning to his face and the worried look dissipated from his face. Stone continued carefully, not wanting his buddy to go into shock again. Stone had never seen his friend that shook before. It almost scared him.

"What I was going to say was that guy Ryker wants a rematch. He heard you had begun training again, and he wants to prove himself. The word is that your head was not in the game, and he got lucky. I don't call it lucky. I mean, he almost killed you. So, I'm sure you know that I would prefer it if you don't take him up on it. Not that I don't believe in you, I just don't want to ever see you that way again. You are my brother, and I love you, man. Well, I did my part. I told you all about it, and now we can forget about it, right?"

Stone was not that crazy to think it would be that easy. But he couldn't help trying it, though.

"Wait a minute, hold up, brother. I think I need to do this. I need to redeem myself."

"You have nothing to prove to anyone, Brick. You were an amazing fighter, and you were getting yourself back on your feet after being knocked down. What he did is not excusable. It isn't surprising that 2 years later, people are still questioning his qualifications. It has to bother him. Otherwise, he would have moved on as well."

That night had changed so much in Brick's life. He lost more than the match, and the other things he could not get back no matter if he did win a rematch against Ryker. A part of him thought he lost a piece of Shae that night as well. She never said anything, but Brick knew all too well that some things do not need to be said to be understood.

"Stone, you know I will not be able to do this without you. If I did not think that I needed it, I would not bother, but I truly think it will help to get the part of me that died that night back. I lost my self-respect for a bit. Man, I spiraled, started using drugs. Something in my psyche was fractured. You know, the demons I constantly fight. You and Shae were there to witness it all firsthand. Man, I need your help to get my life back."

Stone heard his friend as he pleaded with him to take some time and consider all of the potential implications. His heart was heavy, and he hoped that he was doing the right thing by cosigning to help him train for the fight.

"You sure you don't want to talk it over with Shae first?" Stone probed.

"Let's get started, and I will talk it over with her tonight when I get home. I'm sure she will be fine as long as I'm out of her hair."

"You underestimate that woman greatly, dude."

Stone walked over to the punching bag. He always started there. Brick followed, and they began their long day of training with some breaks in between to work with other clients.

Brick was a bit nervous with anticipation of the fight that would eventually come. He would not survive if he did not come out on top, and he feared he would not live it down with Shae, especially since it is his idea to take the fight. He hoped that the preparations for the fight would distract him from the troubles in his marriage.

Brick decided to take an ice bath before heading home. The day had all but passed by. He was so into the training and getting himself psyched up that he did not realize how late it was. Just 15 minutes in the ice bath, he told himself, then he would go home with a clear mind.

After filling the tub up with ice and water, he

immersed himself in it. He never quite understood how it soothed him when most other gym patrons could not handle it for 5 minutes. Laying his head back, he tried to clear his thoughts, but he kept getting images of the fight 2 years ago. No matter how much he tried to picture something happier, that was all he got.

"Babe, Babe, talk to me. Answer me, dammit," Shae screamed out while standing over him.

At that moment, he was lying there on a stretcher, being taken into the operating room for emergency surgery. The look on her face scared him more than anything at the time. That was a feeling he never wanted to repeat. Darkness enveloped him, and he was out for a few days. That night changed everything.

He knew he was out for a few days because Shae and Stone, both told him so, and they told him they were worried he would not make it back, but he survived. He learned a lot from that fight. Also, with that fight, there came many negatives, the night sweats, PTSD episodes. Countless nights of waking up and Shae was sitting in the corner of the room balled up because he was having nightmares and was fighting in his sleep. After almost two years, they started easing up. He went and saw a few therapists to help him get a hold on life. He had withdrawn himself from the gym because he thought he had failed, not only himself but Stone as well.

This ice bath was anything but relaxing. His mind was plagued by so many memories. He knew the only way to fix it was to fight.

Chapter Four

SHAE

Shae was in the bedroom but heard the key turn in the door. Brick walked in, trying to be quiet, but it was too late. She was standing there, and she was not happy. Shae started in on him without pause.

"What are you doing? Do you know what time it is, Brick?"

"You know I was at the gym."

"Were you? I don't know. That is part of the problem. We did not talk all day. You think you can keep coming and going whenever you want with no regard to me? That isn't what we signed up for. At least I didn't. Who all was at the gym?"

"Are you serious right now? What in the world is going on? You know I was at the gym. That is the only place I go if I'm not home. That is the only other place I feel as if I belong. I have never stepped out on you. I have never compromised myself when it comes to our marriage."

"Babe, I know. I know. I just worry about us sometimes. I'm tired of fighting. I just wanted to spend time with you. I thought you were going to be home early enough for us to hang out like we used to," Shae revealed at the end of her rant.

"Shae, I love you, and it has been a long day. I just want to go to bed."

Shae had been standing in his way, blocking his passage through the hall. She moved aside to allow him room to pass. A long sigh escaped her lips as he made his way to the bedroom, and he shut the door.

A few moments later, she heard the showerhead turn on in the bathroom. A part of her wanted to let him be, but the woman in her just could not. She gave him a few moments to himself before she joined him in the shower, wearing her nightie.

Brick started to protest, but he gave in. He missed his wife and their lovemaking. Shae was very loving, and it had been a while since they connected on this level.

She reached for the washcloth so she could wash his back. He handed it to her along with the body wash. This was the kind of thing he had missed more than ever. Shae started at his neck, moving her way down his back with the lather-infused washcloth. She could feel him tense up a little with anticipation. When she finished with his back, she moved to the front and washed his chest down to his abdomen. Shae smiled to herself when she felt him suck in his almost nonexistent stomach. That was one of the parts of him that drove her crazy. When she was finished, she bent her head and placed a kiss dead center in his tickle spot. No matter what, she always seems to be able to zero in on it. She wrung the cloth out as she stood and locked eyes with him as she resoaked the cloth. When she was satisfied, she stooped down again, this time going further so that she could wash his legs. She paused so that her face was just inches away from his manhood, and she blew. She knew he felt it because he shifted.

"Careful love, I'm working here. Surely you wouldn't want to put my eye out."

She continued scrubbing his legs outside and in. When she was content, she washed his private area. Shae ensured that she took her time in this area. She is his wife. After all, it is her job to make sure he is well taken care of. She then made her way towards his tight, well-toned butt. As soon as she touched the cloth to his rear, he grabbed her hand.

"Babe, I got it from here," Brick said with labored breathing.

"But I was enjoying myself," Shae said with a pout.

"Yeah, I know. So was I."

Shae stood and removed her nightie and began washing. Brick told her he would see her in the room when she was done and excused himself. He grabbed his towel and dried off enough to leave the bathroom. After tying the towel around his waist, he went into the kitchen, grabbed a bottle of wine and two glasses, and went off to the bedroom. He poured them both a glass and then he finished drying off and laid down on the bed.

She emerged from the bathroom about 10 minutes later, wrapped in nothing other than her towel. She found Brick sleeping peacefully as she sipped from her wineglass. *Why couldn't it be like this always?* She did not have the heart to wake him up. So, she decided to allow him to sleep. To be honest, she was happy just to lay with him. She slid into bed, and he moved to position his arm so that he was holding her. She fell asleep within a few moments with a smile on her face.

"What the hell?" Brick yelled out.

Brick sat straight up in the bed as he fought to focus his eyes. He saw a look of frustration on Shae's face. She never quite knew what to do other than try to hold him until he calmed down. That is, if he even allowed her to.

"Babe, come here. Let me hold you."

Brick was hyperventilating, his breathing was out of control. This one was pretty bad. Shae watched as he fought in his sleep. As soon as she felt the first jerk, she put enough distance between them. She knew that he would never hurt her on purpose, but there had been a few incidents in the past. One of his episodes left her with a black eye early on after his release from the hospital. She had no choice but to sit and watch as he fought through it. Shae used to call his name and touch him to snap him out of the hold the dream had on him, but she was told to allow it to finish. Otherwise, he may strike her or worse.

As he focused on her, his breathing evened out. He hated that she had to endure his demons with him. Shae tried to hold him, but he wasn't with it.

"I'm good."

"Babe, you know I have your back always, but things are not fine. That episode was worse than before. Are you taking your medications?"

"Dammit, Shae, I don't need you babying me. And no, for the record, I forgot to take it the last few days, but I will be okay as soon as I get it back in my system."

"What can I do, Brick?"

“Honestly, just back off. I told you; I will be fine. You have to watch as I go through this, I apologize. I get it if you want out.”

How dare he. Shae had never once left his side. She felt the words as he said them, and they made her cringe.

Chapter Five

BRICK

Damn, I hate putting her through this. I know that she deserves better.

Brick reached over to turn on the lamp. Of course, she was sitting there looking at him with her loving eyes. He began to get dressed. He pulled on his boxer briefs, sweatpants, and t-shirt. Brick grabbed his keys off the dresser and headed towards the door.

"Where are you going?" Shae asked with a concerned look etched on her features.

"I'll be back. Just chill. I'm good, I promise."

"You might be good, Brick, but I'm not. We cannot go on like this. We were doing good for a whole 3 hours," she said as she looked at her watch.

Without another word, Brick was out the door

and getting into the car. *Man, what are you doing? You are just going for broke.* His phone rang and broke his thoughts. Without looking, he knew it was Shae. Who else would it be at this time of night? He let it go to voicemail. He knew he was hurting her, but he could not stop himself.

He arrived at the gym a few moments later and was relieved that no one else was there. After all, the sun had not come up yet.

Man, this was only going to get worse. If I'm flipping out now, how am I supposed to tell her I'm going to fight soon? The kicker was, it's not just a regular fight. He would be fighting Ryker again. Shae was not going to like this at all. I know I need to tell her sooner rather than later, but how? Brick, you are a world-class jerk. Most guys would kill to have a woman like Shae by his side. Why does she have to push me? Why does she have to accuse me of cheating? I have never been more loyal than I am to her. He kept up the deluge of tumultuous thoughts as he went through his normal warm-up routine.

As Brick made his way to the bag. He knew he had some frustrations to work out. He began taking his frustrations out blow by blow. His punches started out slow and precise. About 30 punches in, he began to pick up the pace, throwing combinations. Each punch was full of force. He continued punching for over an hour. When he was done, the bag held an imprint from his fist. After his assault was over with the bag, he decided to shadow box with himself. He was his own worst enemy, after all.

It was not long before his mind went in its own direction. *Why does Shae continue to stay with me knowing that I'm damaged? Why would she want a man she has to take care of all the time or one she needs to fear sleeping next to? What if I had hurt her this time?* Brick slams his hands against his head. *No more not taking the meds, no matter what is going on. I'm so sorry, Shae.*

He continues rotating between boxing and practicing take-down moves for another 3 hours. Brick knew that Shae should have left for work by now. He would get to avoid her and the anguished look in her eyes for a little while longer. He made it back home to shower and grab something to eat. Brick was mentally worn out, and he decided to nap before heading back to the gym.

Before leaving, he took the time to write Shae a note to let her know he would be at the gym if she needed anything. He put the note on the refrigerator because he knew she would head there first for a drink of water when she arrived home. He knew how he was acting was wrong, but he did not want to deal with it right now.

Chapter Six

SHAE

If only I did not love that man so damn much. I promise I would strangle him. How difficult would it be for him to sit down and say, "Shae, we need to fix this." I'm going to have to be the bigger person and figure it out. I know he loves me. There is no doubt in my mind. Something is going on, but I cannot put my finger on it. I hate it when he goes through these episodes. This one seemed more intense; he was really angry. Maybe I need to call his doctor.

Shae made it to the office well before it was time to meet up with The Punisher at his childhood home. She needed to grab the notes she left accidentally when leaving the day before. She quickly briefed Cassandra on what she was up to, and then she is off. Looking at her watch, she estimates she may have just enough time to beat him there unless he was already there. On the drive over, her mind started going back.

The Punisher has a fight coming up in a few nights that I am sort of obligated to attend. Maybe I can use that as a date night. It has been ages since we have had one of those. I miss nights like last night. At least he held me, and that was refreshing. It is as if our paths are going in separate directions. I am always coming, and he is going. We are like two trains passing in the night.

Shae thought she was going to make it to the location before The Punisher. No such luck. He was there with his entourage in tow.

"Hi," she greeted him with a smile as she parked her car.

"Good morning, gorgeous one, so glad you could make it."

"It's my job. Of course, I was going to make it. Just make sure you keep it on a purely professional level."

"Yeah yeah, I gotcha. Shall we begin?"

Shae did not exactly trust him, but she needed this to work. She needed this story to go off without a hitch. The publicity alone would add another boost to her career.

The walkthrough tour of The Punisher's childhood home went well, and when they were just about ready to leave, he called her to come back and look at something. His crew had gone ahead as well as her cameraman. Shae did not want to be rude. Although she had an uneasy feeling, she still went back inside. Punisher tried to get her to look back as he pointed something out so that he could catch her off guard and pull her into him. Shae caught herself.

"Really? I think we are done here," Shae yelled as she shoved past him. She was beyond flustered and disgusted. A girl could not even do her job without someone trying to come on to her. Pulling out her phone as she exited the building, she called Cassandra.

Cassandra's phone went straight to voicemail.

Hi there, you know what to do. Leave me a message, and I'll get back to you soon.

"Cassandra, this is Shae. Please return my call as soon as you get this. Thanks"

As she was hanging up, she heard her name being called.

"Shae, Shae, wait up. Please..." It was Punisher.

Shae turned and looked at him with coldness in her eyes. She had nothing to say to him. How dare he try anything, especially when she had set him straight before, or so she thought.

"What could you possibly want except for me to ruin your fighting career before it even gets off the ground?"

"Listen, I know I shouldn't have done that. You have to understand I'm used to girls throwing themselves at my feet, and you didn't even bat an eye."

"See, that's the problem. You are used to girls, sweetheart. I am, at most times, a happily married woman. And before you even ask, the other times, we are just fine. It was not an opening for you to try and swoop in. Just grown-up enough to be honest with you."

"I get it. You are married, and more so, you are faithful. Can you say the same for him?"

"Without a doubt in my mind, I can. As a matter of fact, you can ask him yourself when you meet him. We will be at your fight."

"Oh, that is cold-blooded, sweetheart. You going to flaunt your man in front of me? I get it. I get it. You are taken, and you are good with it. I will not disrespect you or him again. Are we cool?"

"Yeah, we cool. I will get the interview finalized and ready to go, and as soon as it is, I will let you know so that we can walk through it together to make sure we are both good with it. Deal?"

"Sounds great, Shae, and again my apologizes, but you are just so fine and cool to be around."

Shae nodded and turned to walk away towards her car. Opening the door, she turns to look back at him and shakes her head wryly as she gets in her car.

Instinctively, she checked her phone to see if Brick had texted or if Cassandra had responded. No luck on either front.

She drove by the office to drop off the footage they shot today and headed for home. She wanted to be there when Brick came in.

Shae made it home in time to get dinner started while she showered and sipped on some red wine. Shae noticed the note from Brick immediately that he left on the fridge secured with the "I Apologize" magnet. Even when he could not find the words, he still did. A smile escaped Shae's lips.

She made spaghetti with meatballs for dinner. It was one of Brick's favorites. Shae brought out the candlesticks and set the table to resemble their first date at Luigi's, their favorite Italian restaurant. She went all out and made garlic cheese breadsticks to go along with the pasta, and for dessert, she had picked up a peach cobbler and vanilla ice cream. Her intention was to have a romantic night, just the two of them. It seemed as if the last one was too far out of memory. She was trying with all her might to rectify it.

As if on cue, Brick turned the lock with the key entering with a worn look on his face. He tried to correct it when he noticed that Shae had gone all out with dinner.

"Wow, babe, ummmm, I'm speechless, well, almost. Dinner looks exceptional," he says as he walks over to where she was standing. He kisses her on the lips fully, but he does not allow his lips to linger. Shae moves to sit down.

"Babe, do you mind if I shower really quick?" he asked, knowing she was going to insist he eat it first so the food would not get cold.

"It is up to you. I'm just glad you are home in time to eat. Food is better when it is hot, though," she said half-jokingly.

Brick went and put his gym bag away and washed his hands and came back and sat down at the table without further hesitation. Shae had begun fixing his plate and was sitting it down as he took his seat.

"Looks and smells great, babe. Thank you for doing this. It all looks so nice, kind of reminds me of Luigi's even down to the tablecloth."

Shae was in shock. She had not expected him to notice that. *Maybe there is some hope for us after all,* she thought to herself. As they made small talk over dinner, Shae felt inclined to tell him more about this project she had been working on.

"You know, I've been working on this interview with The Punisher, right?"

"Yeah," Brick answered with less enthusiasm than she had.

"Listen, I know you are not impressed with him, and he is young, but I was wondering if you would like to go with me to his fight? We have a few nights to think about it."

"If it means that much to you. Yeah, of course, I will go. Just keep me posted on when. I will even dress in my best for you," he smiled as he said it.

Even though he was being sarcastic, Shae was happy he had agreed to go. This would be a step in the right direction of getting their life back on track. Shae had been trying for the last few weeks unsuccessfully to go on a date with her husband, but he was not cooperating. She had not told him that was what she was trying to do, so this time she decided to switch it up and do so. She was happy he agreed, but she knew it was not what he would love to be doing. Shae knew that asking him to be happy and thrilled about it was asking for too much. She decided to take the win and work with that.

Shae began to clear the dishes from the table after they finished eating. Brick came up behind her at the sink and allowed his front to press against her back. A soft moan escapes Shae's lips as Brick turns her head towards him and places a deep kiss on her lips. Just as she began to turn her body to feel him against her, he pulled back.

"I'm going to go and shower, alright?"

Shae was half expecting him to say that he would meet her in the bedroom when she finished, but that did not happen. He went to shower, and she went and climbed into bed. By the time he came out of the shower, she was sleeping, snoring up a storm. He kissed her on the lips, but she was too far gone to even stir. Brick turns to head for the kitchen to grab a beer but notices she has already put his beer and a bottle of water on the bedside table. *She truly was the best. Always thinking of others before herself.* Brick knew he was lucky to have her. He decided right then and there that he would make it more of a point to spend time with her and work on their relationship. He climbed into bed, and before long, he too was sleeping soundly.

Chapter Seven

BRICK

The next morning when Brick awakened, Shae was already up, dressed, and gone. He showered and dressed and headed to the gym. When he arrives, Stone is already there, warming up.

"You ready?" He calls out to Brick as soon as he slips into the door.

"Man, will you ever let up?"

"If you really want to, but then that means you have to leave the gym. You know that is not my style. If we are doing it, we are doing it. No half-stepping. So, you with me?"

"Ughhhh yeah, man. Why are you so serious this fine morning?" Brick looked at Stone, raising his eyebrow.

"Nothing, just thinking I probably shouldn't have

told you. I'm not sure that you will be ready. I mean, did you even talk to Shae about it yet?"

Stone knew the answer before he asked the question. Shae had yet to call and go off on him, so he was certain he had not discussed it with her.

"I'll tell her when it's right."

"When it's right? What, when you are in the cage? That is a little harsh, bro. She deserves better than that. Just talk to her."

"So now you, the great Stone, is giving out advice for those in relationships," Brick regretted that comment as soon as he said it.

"Yeah, I am, actually. My job in life is to teach. But hey, if you think you can do it on your own, cool. All I'm saying is you know as well as I do. You need her in your corner completely." Stone turned and walked away from Brick and started punching the punching bag. It was at that moment that Brick knew he had indeed messed up.

The rest of the day, Brick didn't offer much conversation towards Stone, nor did he. They kind of stayed in their mutual corners of the gym, still training and working, but with some tension. Brick knew he needed to apologize but being the stubborn man, he was he refused.

Brick decided to leave the gym earlier than

normal and head home. He thought it was better if he put some distance between him and Stone.

Stone continued chatting it up with the other members and working out with his clients, showing he was unbothered. A part of him wanted to grab Brick up and lay his hands on him, but he knew that wouldn't help. He knew he had to exercise patience with him.

Over the next few days, the men seemed to get back to speaking and had moved on from the slight disagreement. Stone was working Brick out again, and he could see the progress that he had made.

"You are coming along pretty nicely," Stone complimented Brick.

"Thanks, man. You put me on a time-out, so I had to make it worth it. My hard work does not stop. I have to be ready."

"This time, you will be. I'm going to see to it. You should go home and get some rest. You have been going pretty hard."

"Yeah, you are probably right. Shae has texted me a few times about dinner."

Brick puts out his fist for a fist bump from Stone before telling him that he would catch him later.

Brick headed to the locker, grabbed his belongings, and was just about to head towards the door when he caught a glimpse of The Punisher on the TV.

So that is the punta that Shae is interviewing. He looks soft. His phone vibrated with a text from Shae.

Bring home some lettuce for the salad if you are coming home anytime soon.

Always, Shae

Brick called her instead of texting to let her know he would be home shortly. He could hear the joy in her voice as she went over the menu.

He arrived home in record time. The store was, for once, not busy. He got in and out in a matter of moments, whereas normally, he would end up being in there for a minimum of thirty minutes.

Pulling up to the house, he sat in the driveway a moment before getting out. Shae was extra nice, so he was unsure of what to expect. His thoughts were interrupted as she turned on the porch light and stood, brow quirked at the door, with her arms folded across her chest. Waiting for him to come inside. Brick exited the car, reaching over to grab the bag of groceries from the passenger seat, mindful of locking the door behind him. That was a mistake he had made twice, and both times he came out to find his car had been rummaged through and his loose cash was all gone. Thankfully, there was no damage to his vehicle either time. Each time, he had received a verbal bashing from his wife.

"You know that isn't safe. What if they had taken

something more important? For all you know, they could have been waiting for you in the morning to hurt you. How am I supposed to live with that?" Shae yelled out.

As he walked to the door, Shae opened the door to greet him. She grabbed the bag and planted a kiss on his lips.

"Hi Babe, I'm so glad you made it home at a decent time," smiling as she was saying it. The one thing Shae did not want to happen was for him to get ill about anything. All she wanted was a night of peace and just love. "Dinner will be done by the time you get comfortable; I just have to do the salad mainly and a few odds and ends."

Brick smiled and headed for the bedroom, stripping his clothes off as he went. Shae turned just in time to catch a glimpse of his naked body. Thoughts began to fill her head. Maybe dinner could wait a little while longer. *That man still turns me on.* Shae decided to wait until he was in the shower for a few minutes, and then she would join him.

Brick placed his dirty clothes in the hamper located outside the bathroom, grabbed a fresh towel from the linen closet, and made his way to the shower. He turned the water on so that it could get nice and hot while he brushed his teeth and washed his face.

Meanwhile, in the kitchen, Shae hurriedly made the salad and turned the oven down low to keep the steaks nice and juicy while she ventured to try to entice her husband for a little foreplay.

Shae strips down to her birthday suit and gently taps on the door. When Brick did not answer, she tapped lightly again. Receiving no response, she opened the door gently and hit the dimmer on the light switch before opening the door to the shower. Before Brick could protest, she was inside with her mouth on his. Pulling away slightly, she wanted to make sure he was good; she received her answer as he pulled her to him and reclaimed her mouth. Brick's hands roamed from the small of her back down to cup her plump butt, and then he moved to her thighs, giving them a gentle squeeze. Shae moaned in his ear. That was all it took as he spread her legs and entered her. Her hips began to gyrate against him. After the initial sensation, his rhythm matched hers perfectly. Shae planted kisses to his chest and took his right nipple into her mouth. She switched between sucking it and gently biting it. She knew this was one of his weaknesses and she exploited it. His pace began to quicken as he thrust inside of her honey pot. Generally, Brick would take his time, but there was so much pent-up frustration he thrusted deeper inside, wanting to fill her with all of him. When he felt himself on the verge of exploding, he grabbed her a little tighter. She could feel the muscles within his thighs as they flexed.

"Shae!"

"Yes, my love," she answered as she dug her nails into his back.

"I c... can't hold it," he stammered.

"I know," Shae replied as she clinched her muscles around his love stick and quickly released them. "It's okay to release my love."

"Oh, my G..G....God woman. I love you," he yelled out as he filled her with his essence.

Feeling satisfied with herself, Shae kissed him fully and deeply and separated herself from him while looking him in his eyes. She never understood exactly why that turned him on as well, but it always did. She reached behind him for her washcloth and poured a few drops of Dove Cucumber Melon shower gel onto it and handed it to him for him to wash her back.

"So, you think I'm just going to wash your back, and that is it, huh?"

"Mmmmhhhhmm"

"How are you so sure?"

"Because you know I have dinner in the oven," she smiled as the water was tapping on her back. She turned away from him, so her back was now to him.

"Baby, please wash my back and only my back. I will get the rest."

Brick sighed but obliged as his manhood throbbed, wanting more. But he knew he should wait. He washed her back, ensuring that he took his time. Shae could tell he was extra deliberate with each wipe. She felt the cloth barely touching her skin. *Oh, he thinks he is slick. Not today, Brick. Not today.* As much as she hated to leave him alone in the shower, knowing that he was longing for her, she turned and kissed him fully on the lips as she opened the shower door. She took her time stepping out, knowing that she was tempting him even further.

"I'll see you when you're done, babe. No need to hurry. Dinner still has a few more minutes before it is ready", Shae winked as she spoke.

"Yes, ma'am," Brick threw in a salute.

Brick did not take long before he came out of the bathroom, all clean and fresh. He went into the room and dried himself off, throwing on his Yoda pajama pants and a t-shirt, and made his way into the dining room. Shae was about to pull out the steaks from the oven when Brick walked up behind her. She turned her head as he started dancing against her, unable to help but sway with him. When he wanted to be, he was irresistible. Brick nuzzled her neck. This is what Shae missed more than anything. The good times, simple but good. Shae missed him, showing her that he was still in love with her.

"Babe, come on, let us eat, and then we can play. Maybe."

Brick went and sat down as Shae brought the steaks to the table and grabbed the asparagus and salad from the fridge. Before sitting down, she grabbed a bottle of their favorite Chardonnay to complement the meal.

Brick smiled to himself. If he had anything to do with it, round two was coming. If there is one thing everybody knows, it is that Shae could not hold her alcohol. Brick had to admit he had often taken advantage of the very situation at times. Of course, not against her will or anything, but just because she was more open to exploring when intoxicated.

Shae tosses around the idea of bringing up the fight, but the night was going so well she didn't want to risk anything upsetting Brick. Sometimes it was frustrating walking around on eggshells, but what else could she do? She loved him.

The pair made quick work of their dinner. They talked about their day. Shae wanted to tell him about the incident with the punisher, but she knew that would change the way the night was going. She hated keeping secrets from him.

Shae stood up and backed away from the table slowly. Bricked smiled, "Oh no, you don't."

Laughing, Shae replied, "Oh, but you know the rules, my love. I've let you get by a few times, but you know what has to happen."

Brick reared back in his chair, folding his arms across his chest, pretending to pout. Shae always had the hardest time resisting that adorable face. Although he has been through a lot, he had a baby-face. Usually, he kept his face clean and cut. The guys at the gym always gave him a rough time, but he did not care.

"Babe, come on. I'm tired. I just want to lay down now that I got my belly full."

"Oh, I see, so no round two, right? You know the deal. I cook, you clean," she teased.

"Wait—wait for a second, umm, can we negotiate this?" Brick smiled at his wife while sticking his lips out.

"You are lucky I love you. If you get the kitchen taken care of by the time I get out of the shower, and I mean if, perhaps we can consider a round two." Shae turned and began to leave the kitchen, making sure to switch her hips as she walked away. Without looking back, she knew she was being watched. She sighed to herself. You still got it, girl.

Feeling defeated, Brick began to clear the table so

that he could get the dishes done. He piled the dishes up near the sink. The leftovers he placed in plastic storage containers and put them in the fridge. Brick ran the dishwater, adding a little Dawn dish detergent to the water. He placed the dishes in the sink to soak for a few while he cleaned the kitchen. Brick was mindful to wipe the table and the stove. He knew his wife. One thing other than the fact she loved him; she hated a dirty kitchen.

Shae's thoughts shifted to her mom, Isabella. That was something her mom instilled in her from an early age. Shae smiled. This was the first time she thought of her mom in a while. She missed her more than she let on. Her mom passed away a few years ago right after she lost the baby.

Her thoughts stayed with her mom as she took her shower. She didn't hear as Brick entered the bathroom. She was almost embarrassed when he opened the door to see tears streaming down her face along with the water. Shae jumped as he had startled her.

"Babe, what's wrong? I thought we were having a good time tonight," Brick asked, showing his concern by turning the water off and pulling her into his powerful embrace.

"I'm just...just... missing my mom," Shae sighed and exhaled deeply.

Although she hated feeling broken around her husband, she welcomed his tenderness.

Brick grabbed her towel and helped her to get out of the shower. He began drying her off. He started with her face, careful to wipe her tears away. Instead of drawing this out, he made quick work of the process and wrapped the towel around her. Brick then picked her up and carried her to their bedroom and gently placed her on the bed. Brick climbed into bed with her, sliding up close to her so he could cuddle with her. Pretty soon, he felt her body relax. He knew she had fallen asleep, that made it easier for him to do the same.

A few days later, Shae wakes up and is her normal self. She is in the kitchen making breakfast when Brick walks in and places a kiss on her upturned lips. This was one part of their day that they were both starting to grow accustomed to once again. The past week had been full of surprises within their private life.

"Babe, you do remember that tonight is our date night, right?"

"Yeah, yeah. I remember. Are we still going to watch that fight?"

"Um yeah. Brick, you promised we could do this."

"Yeah, I know Shae. That doesn't mean I have to be thrilled. I mean come on. You want me to be happy about someone else living their dream in the ring? I get it though Shae, this isn't only my world, it's yours too. I will be there. Are we meeting up here or do you just want me to meet you there?"

"There is fine, babe. I've got some errands to run and some things to take care of at the office, but I will be looking for you. I know this is hard. I guess I didn't realize just how hard it was until now. If you want to opt out, just say the word."

"I said I would go Shae!"

When Brick turned and walked out of the kitchen there was no, I love you called out. He knew she was mad, and in a way, he wanted it to be that way. If she was pissed, there would be more anger seen in her eyes than that of disappointment or pity for her husband. Brick admitted to himself that his view was often skewed when it came to him. None of that stopped him from getting dressed and heading to the gym. His one true sanctuary.

Once he steps inside the gym, he gets lost in the environment. He wastes no time beginning his pre workout warmups while he waited for his workout partner, Stone.

Chapter Eight

SHAE

That man of mine, ughhhhhhh I could just choke him sometimes. Why does he have to be so freaking difficult? All he had to say was, "Shae, I'd rather not go to the fight if that is okay?" I mean, of course I would have been disappointed, but I get it. Yet he agreed. Now he is going to show up being a jerk. I'm not sure why I'm not used to his behavior by now.

Shae has always tried to make sure they never parted ways with harsh words or if they did, she would always be the one to call or text to try and fix it. This time, she did not. She truly did not see what was so wrong about wanting to spend time with her husband. He was training at the gym, so why would she feel like he could not watch a fight? That man drives her bonkers.

{{{{BUZZ BUZZ}}}}

Shae's phone rang as she turned the key in the

ignition and waited for the phone to connect to the car, before answering it.

"Cassandra, hi, how is it going?"

"Going great as far as I know, Shae. Were you able to get that piece wrapped up so it will be ready tomorrow? No better time than when there is this buzz right after his fight tonight. You are going tonight, right?" Cassandra questioned.

"Yes, ma'am, I wouldn't miss it. I worked hard on this piece and if there is anything, I can add to make it better than I will."

"Good, I may just see you there myself. I have a date," Cassandra giggled into the phone.

It was good to hear the laughter in Cassandra's voice. It was even better to know she had a date. Cassandra had lost her husband to prostate cancer a few years earlier, and she had taken it hard. There were no children for her to lean on, so she leaned on Shae. Cassandra had become fond of Shae when she first came to work with her. Richard, Cassandra's husband, often joked that Shae and Brick were the children they never had.

"Yessssss, it's about time. Make sure you tell whomever this man is, your children don't play about you. He better come correct."

"You are funny, Shae. Hopefully, I will see you and Brick there this evening."

"Yes, ma'am, we shall be there. It is our date night as well. Although we had a disagreement this morning, hopefully it will still be a great night for everyone."

Cassandra assured her it would be, before hanging up to take another call.

Shae pulled out of her driveway and headed towards the office. She wanted to grab her notes and go back over the article to put some semi finishing touches on it. Shae had always been a bit of a perfectionist and it showed in her work. She was the recipient of several awards throughout her career.

After a full day of errands and cleaning up her story, Shae heads home to get dressed. Shae didn't find too many things to dress up for these days, so she never disappointed when the opportunity rose. A few weeks ago, when she began planning for her date night surrounding the fight, she had gone shopping. She was beyond excited when she spotted the sheath off the shoulder Asymmetrical Chiffon cocktail dress with ruffles in peacock. If it were in jade that would have been better but, she had just the shoes that would complement this dress just fine. Shae squealed when the sales associate told her it was on sale.

Shae stripped down and headed for the bathroom to take a quick shower. She still had to do her hair, which was going to take at least an hour. Her hair hung down to her mid-back and was naturally curly. The last few days she had been simply pulling her hair up into a messy bun to keep from having to do it, but that would not work for tonight. Although it was a fight, anytime Shae was out with Brick, she made sure she looked a certain way. It wasn't about the attention she received, but more about making sure Brick was represented well.

{{{{BUZZ BUZZ}}}}

Shae's phone was going off, and it broke her concentration. She walked over to check it. A part of her wished it was Brick checking in. No such luck.

The text that came through was from The Punisher.

I can't wait to see you tonight. Wish me luck.

Shae responded quickly and then threw the phone onto the bed.

I'm sure you will do just fine. No luck is needed.

Shae continues doing her hair. She then makes herself a quick sandwich before getting dressed. Upon entering the bedroom, she picked her phone up with a little attitude and sent a text to Brick's phone. She held onto the phone for a moment, expecting him to reply right back. She wasn't surprised when he wasn't.

This is ridiculous. Stop your whining, Shae. He said he

would meet you there. No need to stress yourself out over what is supposed to be a good night all around.

After applying the finishing touches to her hair, she grabbed her jacket and headed out of the door. The fight was due to begin in an hour. Shae was thankful that her parking space was secured. There were a lot of people in attendance, she noticed as she arrived at the coliseum.

Smiling to herself, they love their hometown celebs. Shae parked her car and was escorted inside to the VIP section. Cassandra and her date were already there.

"Shae, my dear. This is Austin. Austin, this is my best journalist Shae. She also doubles as my daughter occasionally."

Austin extended his hand out to Shae, as he did so Shae began to analyze him. He was a little taller than Cassandra. He had dark eyes that seemed to pull one in. His handshake was firm, and he never broke eye contact. He was noticeably younger than Cassandra, but it was not her place to judge. As her eyes moved from Austin to Cassandra, she could see the happiness in Cassandra.

As Shae was shaking Austin's hand, she leaned in and whispered, "Don't hurt this woman. She is very near and dear to me."

Austin nodded in agreeance and smiled. Shae

noticed that he sported a few gold teeth. It gave him a rugged look. She approved.

"Darling, where is Brick?"

"He is supposed to be here. Perhaps he got held up," Shae said, shrugging her shoulders.

Just then, a bottle of wine was brought to the table, along with glasses. Shae wasted no time in pouring drinks for the table.

Ding.......Ding......

"In the red corner, we have your hometown favorite, The Punisher."

The crowd erupts into cheers. All of this was all too familiar to Shae. She had to admit she missed it.

The fight gets under way. The Punisher is quick on his feet. His movements seem so fluid. He glides across the floor, striking his opponent quickly and efficiently. Then he moves back and goes on the defense. His opponent lands a few face shots before going to work on Punisher's legs.

Ding.......Ding...... the end of round 1

Walking back to his corner, the Punisher locks eyes with Shae and winks at her. She smiles back and gives him a thumbs up. She then moves her pointer finger in a circle, gesturing for him to speed it up. He smiles and nods.

Before long, the second round had begun. Shae was watching Punisher and if she didn't know any better, she would have sworn that it was Brick up there. She pulled her phone from her purse, sighing, still nothing from Brick, she was tempted to message or call him, but she decided against it.

Shae's attention was pulled back to the ring. Punisher did a quick take down of his opponent in the first few seconds of round 3. She had been so preoccupied that she hadn't caught much of round 2. The Punisher had his opponent in a submission hold, and he tapped out.

Ding.......Ding......

"We have a winner," the announcer stated while holding up The Punisher's right hand. Surveying the crowd, he locked eyes with Shae again. He again winked at her. She smiled and clapped her hands after giving him 2 thumbs up.

Shae did not wait around long after the fight ended. She, Cassandra, and Austin made their way to their vehicles moments after the winner was announced.

Cassandra knew that Shae was not in the greatest mood since Brick did not show up. She thought twice about inviting her for drinks, but she did anyway. She did not want Shae to feel rushed off.

"You up for drinks?"

"Well, Cass, I'm so glad that you brought Austin. It was a pleasure to meet you," she said as she turned in his direction. “I’m going to head home. It has been a long day. Drinks sound great but, I’m beat.” Cassandra shook her head in agreement.

“I will see you on Monday morning. Get some rest, and go easy on him,” she whispered in Shae's ear as the two ladies hugged.

The ride home for Shae was done in silence. When she arrived home, she did not even remember getting out of the car and going into the house.

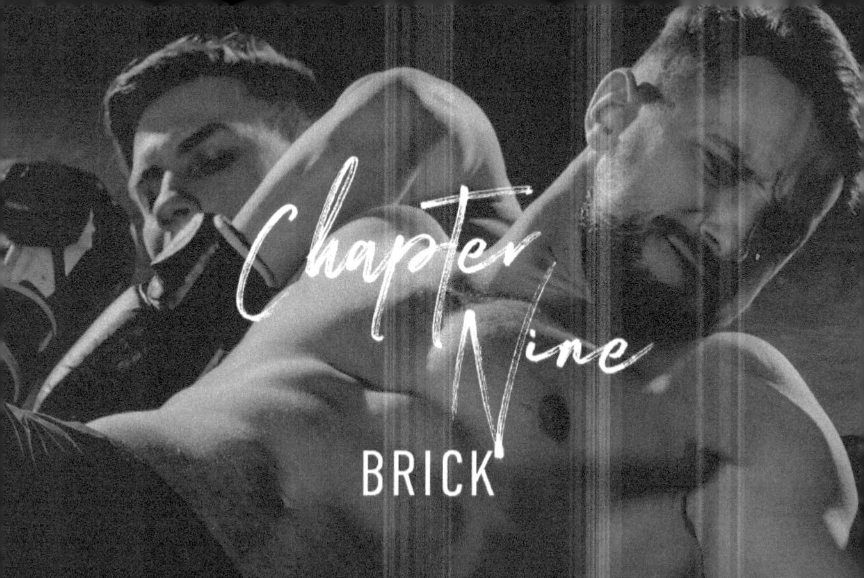

Chapter Nine

BRICK

Looking at his watch, he thought he might be able to get home before Shae. The idea was to be in bed and sleep, to not have to hear the argument he was sure was coming.

The truth was, he had no real reason as to why he blew her off. It would have been so much easier just to say he was not up to it. As he was walking to his car, he scrolled through the unanswered messages he had received. All he could do was shake his head.

"It's about to be a shit storm."

And in other local news, The Punisher won tonight's match, came through the radio. Of all things to hit him when he crank up his car.

Brick's first thoughts were to call up Stone and ask him if he could stay the night. He decided against it. He would have to face her at some point. Besides, he knew Stone would tell him no. Not that he would turn him away if he was in need, but he was not going to be caught in the middle of something with him and Shae. Anyone else, stone would go to war. He was funny like that.

The drive home seemed quicker than normal. That did not help with trying to gather his thoughts.

The house was dark when he pulled up into the driveway. Just maybe she was still out, or even better, sleeping already. He put the key into the door and turned the handle to unlock it and enter. He only stepped two steps in when he heard movement.

"Oh, so you do know where you live, at least."

"Of course, I know where I live, Shae. Stop tripping," Brick replied.

"Tripping! Who me? Or is that a response to your actions of the day?"

Brick turned on the light switch, only to have Shae turn the other side off. Before she did, he was able to see her sitting there with her legs crossed, with a beer in her hand.

"You know, I waited all day to hear from you. I thought maybe you would call or text me to say something. But as the day passed, nothing."

"I lost track of time, Shae."

"Oh yeah, so — my text messages did nothing? To jar your memory of your prior engagement? That you agreed to, by the way," Shae lashed out, emphasizing her words as she spoke.

"All I wanted to do was spend time with you. I guess that makes me a fool, right?"

Brick hung his head down; he knew there was nothing to say. He tried to walk past Shae, thinking the worst was over.

She was not through with him. "How much longer do you think you can continue treating me this way? Do you know how I felt, sitting there looking around for you? Cassandra invited me to hang out for a bit and get drinks."

"So why let me stop you? You should have gone, Shae," Brick yelled out. "Because if you had, I would not be having to listen to this foolishness."

"All I wanted was to spend time with you. I just want us to be like we were. We used to be happy. Now it seems as if you just go through the motions," Shae exhaled and then took a sip of her beer.

"What do you want from me, Shae? I apologize for not showing up. But babe, that's all I got."

Shae could not believe how nonchalant he was being about the whole thing. She began questioning their relationship. She stood up and downed the rest of the beer before walking to the kitchen counter. Car keys in hand, she tried to push past Brick. "I'm leaving!"

"Shae, don't play."

She reached for the door with her right hand, and he grabbed her left arm, pulling her back toward him. It did not go quite as planned and Shae ended up on the floor. She sat there in shock for a moment. When she realized that she was on the floor, she scrambled to get to her feet. Brick reached out to help her, but she pushed his hand away.

"Have you lost your mind?"

"Shae, I'm sorry, okay. Please do not leave. Let's just go to bed. We can revisit it tomorrow with clear heads. I didn't mean for you to fall on the floor. I just wanted you to stop, babe. You know I would never do anything to hurt you."

The keys had fallen out of her hand when she fell to the floor. When she caught sight of the oversized S's blinged in purple glitter, she bent to grab it up. When she did, she fell over. The drink had been her sixth in a short time frame and it was starting to affect her equilibrium. Brick motioned to help her up but that just made it worse. Shae was too tipsy to be embarrassed, but she was still mad. She sat there on the floor and began to cry.

Brick was scared to walk away because he knew she would leave. He did the only thing he could do. He sat down on the floor with her, pulling her close to him.

"It will be okay, Shae, I promise. I'm truly sorry," he whispered in her ear.

Shae cried herself to sleep as Brick continued to hold her. About an hour passed before he felt it was safe to try to move her to the bedroom, which he did with little effort. He placed Shae on the bed and carefully undressed her. He then covered her with the blanket. Brick stood over her for a few moments, taking her in. *How can he be so stupid? Shae has taken so much over these last few years and did it gracefully.* Brick should be thankful that she hung around.

Brick stepped back from the bed, began pulling his shirt over his head. Next, he unzipped his pants and stepped out of them before picking them up and throwing that and his shirt into the clothes hamper.

"Dude, get it together before you lose her," he taunted himself. Brick turned back towards the bed as he heard Shae shifting. Once he felt she had settled back down, he took his shower, eased into bed, and held his wife. He held her as if his life depended on it.

Never until that moment was, he terrified that she would walk away from him. In his heart, he knew he had to come clean to her. His thoughts got the better of him, but finally, sleep came for him.

Chapter Ten

SHAE

Shae wakes to find herself in the bed, with Brick's arm thrown over her. She was still upset as she thought about the events of the previous night. How could she dislike him, yet love him with all her might? She loved his smell. She let out a deep breath as she inhaled his scent in. As she did, she winced with pain. She had not taken the time to notice it until then.

As quietly as she can, she slides out of the bed and heads to the bathroom and takes her shower. Under normal circumstances, she would take this time to reflect. But she hurried to get out of the house before he woke up. A part of her did not want to deal with the drama.

Shae got herself together in record time and headed to the office. Today was Saturday, so hopefully, not many would be there. At least, she hoped. She was not in the mood for chatting.

On the drive to work, Cassandra called.

"How did things go last night? Is Brick still breathing?"

"Cass, last night was not good. I felt like a fool. I mean, what is more important than spending time with your wife, right?"

"Sweetheart, did he offer up a reason? I am certain that he had a good reason why. That man has always been good to you and for you. The two of you remind me of myself and Richard. Without the broad shoulders and the MMA fighting, of course," she laughed as she talked, trying to ease the mood.

Shae was not in the laughing mood, although she knew Cassandra had well intentions. She just wanted her to agree with her more than anything else.

"Listen darling, the move Brick pulled last night was a crap move. But it honestly is not his first one. I know it may seem frustrating right now, but you two will get through whatever this is. Just talk to him"

"That's just it Cassandra, he won't talk. He keeps shutting me out. The more I try, it seems the more bricks he lay down to build his wall up. To be honest, it is beyond exhausting at times," Shae urged.

"Being in a marriage is give and take Shae. And yes, love, I know what you have been through, and I truthfully could not tell you if that is something I would have survived. That alone proves that you two have so much more love to give to one another. I wish my Richard were still here. There is not anything I would not give to have him back for a moment." Cassandra's words trailed off as she began to get lost in her thoughts.

"I'm sorry darling, I seem to have disappeared on you. The way that man can take my thoughts away is the same way I see you when you are with Brick or talking to him. Tell me, does he still take your breath away?"

"Ughhhh, you know he does. But that does not make it right," Shae grumbled.

"All I'm saying is talk to the man," Cassandra's voice trailed off again. "Oops, sorry sweets, I've got to take this call. It's Austin." She sounded happy to hear from him.

"Yes ma'am. I will talk to you later. Have fun."

An hour or so later, Shae has made it to the office and was in her work zone. She could not believe how well the piece was shaping up to be. As she was about to click the send button, there was a knock on the door.

"Come in," she called out.

"Hey Shae, I didn't expect you to be in today," Rodney Matthews, the editor, stated.

"Yeah, well, I had a few more things to add to my piece after watching the fight. What are you doing on a Saturday? Don't tell me Delores is off shopping again."

"You know her spending habits. Someone has to work," he said, laughing.

Shae was smiling as well.

"Since you are here though, why in the world did you not tell us about Brick?"

Shae had a look of confusion on her face. *Could he possibly know about the fight between her and Brick? No freaking way.*

"Ummmm Rodney, you have me lost. What are you talking about?" Shae inquired, without taking her eyes off him.

"Come on now, Shae. You know the fight."

"What fight?"

"Well, maybe rematch would describe it better. The one that is scheduled for three weeks from today." Rodney had turned his back to Shae as he continued to talk. "I was hoping you would work your magic on the piece since you rocked the one on Punisher. I saw the preliminary copy. Great work, as always," he said while turning back to face Shae. It was then that he saw the look of hurt on her face.

Without saying anything, Shae got up, grabbed her bag and in minutes was out the door and in her car.

Rodney was left standing there, not knowing what he just unleashed.

Chapter Eleven

BRICK

Shae did not remember the actual drive to the gym. In her mind, she must have teleported there. Shae chose to go by the gym first, because where else would he be? She was right; she thought as she pulled into a parking space.

Brick was inside working out on the punching bag when Shae walked inside. He heard the door and instinctively looked over. The look on her face was enough to tell him they were about to have part two of the events from last night.

Shae walks up to him, rubbing her head.

"Hey," she says. Brick looks in her direction. "Can we talk? Correction, we need to talk now."

Brick tried to shake her off as she grabbed a hold of his arm as he was throwing a punch to the bag.

"Shae, come on now. Don't do that. We can talk later at home. I'm in the middle of something."

That did not sit well with her.

"That is the problem, at least part of it. You always seem to be in the middle of something when it comes to me. It is funny really. You seem to have time to talk and be with everyone else except me. How could you?"

"Shae, what are you talking about now? How could I do what? It seems like I'm always on the receiving end of you bitchin," Brick turned around to realize he and Shae had an audience.

"I care about you! I show concern. Wondering as to why you signed up to fight Ryker again. Or anyone, for that matter." Shae poked his chest. "How dare you talk to me like this, especially in the presence of others?"

"Shae, stop poking me. You started this. This is what you want. Why do you get to tell me what I can and cannot do? That is not your choice. You cannot dictate that. Either you are here, or you are not. You do not know what it felt like in that ring that night. You don't know!" he screamed and walked away. Brick was boiling mad; he kicked a bench as he made his way to the shower room.

Stone, the owner of the gym, had walked in at the end of that horrible display. He was not too happy with the scene he had happened upon, but he knew it would happen. He told brick to talk to his wife. Stone would have done it himself, but he was trying to respect Brick's wishes.

Chapter Twelve

SHAE

Shae knew she was wrong. Maybe she should not have come here to handle it. He left her no choice. Yet again she is left standing here looking like a fool. Shae was about to turn on her heels and head for the exit when she saw Stone had approached, motioning for her to come with him. At the disappointed look from him, the tears Shae had been holding back rained down.

Stone escorts her to the office. He closes the door once they are inside. Shae takes a seat on the left side of the couch. Stone walks to the fridge and grabs a bottle of Dasani water and hands it to her along with a tissue he grabbed from the desk.

Sitting down, he takes a deep breath.

"Shae, I need you to calm down, please."

She was wiping her tears in between sniffles.

"I'm fine. At least I will be."

"I take it that was about the fight, right?"

Shae nodded.

"I'm sorry that I didn't tell you myself that there was a possibility of it." Stone said, trying to assume some of the blame for this mess.

"You and I both know that he is a grown man. It appears that he has made a decision already to do this, yes?"

Stone nodded.

"Well, there doesn't seem to be much else to say. I have been his cheerleader, his punching bag and I cannot continue taking it. I should not have to. All I have ever done was love him and love him unconditionally."

As Shae spoke, Stone could hear the hurt in her voice. Shae had always been tough, and this bothered him to see. As much as he loved Brick, it was like he had taken all the fight out of her.

"It was hard to pick up the pieces and try to rebuild after that night. I can't go through that," she continued.

"Shae, you know he is going to need you, no matter the outcome. I feel truly awful because I should never have told him that Ryker said that the media never really gave him his props for the fight. He is looking for a chance to prove that he is the champion. Unfortunately, my brother is trying to prove it as well. You, my sister, are getting caught up in the crossfire. I can tell you this with certainty. If you love him, you are going to have to let him fight."

"What if he gets hurt worse, or he dies? Am I just supposed to take it? He is all I have. Help me understand how I am supposed to watch the man I love self-destruct?"

"If you do not, he will continue down this path of destruction. Right now, he feels like a failure. He not only lost a part of himself with the fight, but you also lost your child, and as a man, that can do something to you. He and I have discussed it before. He feels like he is not giving the best of himself to you. The part that was lost was his manhood. He needs to get it back."

"At what cost?"

"Unfortunately, sis, at all costs. I know it is hard, but you must let him go through with it. I know this will not matter much but I have been here and working with him. He is better than he ever was. There are just a few pieces we need to continue working on over the next few weeks. But I honestly believe he can and will do what he needs to. Even if it is not the win, it is a win for him. It means he fought back to get his life back."

"Stone, I get it. I guess, but I cannot be there for him if he continues to push me away. And that is what has been happening at every turn." Shae sounded frustrated as she stood up to leave.

"Shae, you are in no position to drive."

"I can't stay here. I want to go home."

"I'll walk you out if you insist. Listen, you know I love you like a sister. Just be there for him. I promise it is worth it. He will be better when it is over." He paused before beginning again. "I need you to trust me. Can you do it?" He could sense her hesitation. "Come on Shae, please."

"You are asking a lot of me right now. Did you hear how he was speaking to me? He was beyond disrespectful."

"I caught the tail end. Do not worry about it, I will take care of him for that. He knows better," he stated, giving Shae a hug before she walked out of the door. He used his foot to hold for her.

STARTING HER CAR, SHE HEADS IN THE DIRECTION of home. The drive home did Shae some good. She thought that Brick might have gone back into the gym once she went with Stone, but when she got outside, his car was gone. Instinctively, she checked her phone to make sure that she did not have a missed call from him. There was a call from

Cassandra as well as Rodney. She paused long enough to listen to the voice messages.

Hey Shae, Cass, I just wanted to say that I loved the final piece you did on Punisher. You out did yourself. Celebrate, you have earned it. See you on Monday.

Shae, it's me Rodney. I am so sorry that I spoke out of turn. It was not my place to break that to you. I realized the way you left that you did not have a clue. Again, I apologize. Call me back if you need to. Oh yeah, I read the final. Even better than the first draft. Outstanding writing, as always. Okay, bye.

Shae decided against returning the phone calls. She was just not ready to talk to anyone yet. Shae noticed as she pulled into the driveway, Brick was not at home. Instinctively, she sighed. A side of her was grateful, but she began to worry when she walked inside and surveyed the house. He had been there. Walking through the house into the bedroom, she noticed his closet door was open and a few things were falling from their hangers. There were clothes on the floor. Shae turned and walked into the kitchen, turning her attention to the fridge. Sure enough, he had left her a note.

I need some time. I know you mean well. Love you always, Brick.

He kept it short and simple. One thing Shae loved about him.

She grabbed out her phone and was about to dial Stone's number when she saw a text message from him.

Do not worry, he is with me.

Shae smiled as she opened the fridge and grabbed a beer out. At least she knew he would be safe. Stone would never allow Brick to go too far.

Shae made her way to the bathroom to run some bath water. She wanted to soak away the day's troubles. As the water was running, she went into the bedroom and grabbed a shirt he had worn a few days ago that was on the floor. His scent was so strong it was like he was right there as she inhaled deeply before dropping the shirt into the hamper. Shae checked her phone once again before placing it on its charger.

She began to discard her clothing and again went to the bathroom to settle into the tub. The warm water enveloped her and eased her thoughts as she drifted off after a few moments. Conversations from the past filled her mind.

Shae woke about 30 minutes later, all wrinkled. She washed herself off and released the drainer. As the water drained from the tub, she turned on the shower to rinse herself thoroughly before exiting the bathtub.

She grabbed up her warm beer after wrapping her

towel around her and headed to the kitchen. She swapped the warm beer for a fresh ice cold one and headed to her bedroom. Picking up her phone, she checked it once again. There was no message from Brick, but Stone sent a thumbs up sign, to which she replied, "Thank You!!"

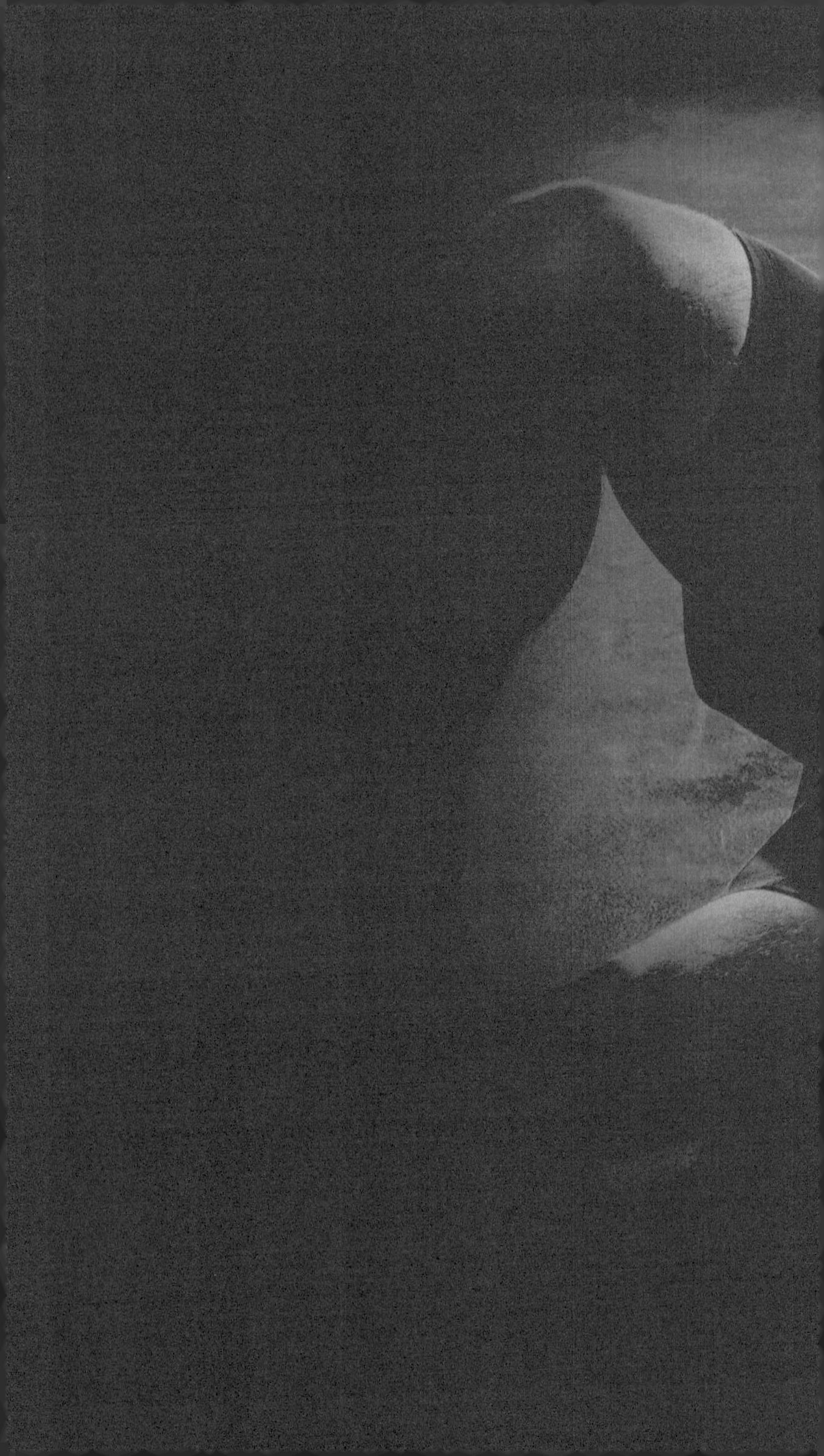

Chapter Thirteen

BRICK

Brick drove around for an hour before deciding to head to the house and grab a few things. He did not want to be there with Shae right now. His emotions were all over the place and it was becoming more and more overwhelming. He had texted Stone to keep her there if he could lessen the chance of running into her.

Brick ended up at the bar across the street from the gym, shooting pool with a few regulars and drinking a few beers to ease his mind. He still could not believe that Shae acted as she did. Brick also knew that he had crossed a line himself. He hated knowing that he hurt her, but she had to understand that he was still a man with pride and who needed to feel like he was whole.

"Hey dude, I figured I would find you here," Stone said, tapping him on the shoulder.

"Man, I don't know what to do. Nah, I take it back; I know what to do, but I do not know how to do it and not have Shae's blessing. It's not as if I want to hurt her."

"I get it. I tried to get her to understand it from your perspective." Stone continued as he picked up a pool stick. "I told her it is just something you have to do. You know she is just worried about you. She saw you through some pretty bad stuff, bro."

Brick exhaled before taking his shot.

"I lost a part of myself."

Stone motions for the server to bring him two cold ones. Cherise is happy to oblige. She is but one of many who has a crush on him.

"Alright bro, after we finish these two, we going to head home so we don't have all these ears listening in," he winked at Brick while saying it.

Brick started sipping on his beer to prolong their time at the bar. "Come on, man, we can play at least two more games. I am finally winning. Tj normally kicks my butt, but tonight I got him on the ropes." Tj just laughed. He was one of the regulars at the gym. He witnessed the drama between Shae and Brick earlier and felt bad, so he decided to take it easy on him.

"You can procrastinate all you like; the conversation is going to occur. We can do it here or at my place. I assume you are coming home with me."

"This is what happens when you put yourself out. I have no choice but to crash at your place. That is if it is okay. I didn't even ask to come to think of it. Knowing you, you might have some hottie coming over," he elbowed Stone as he talked.

"Luckily for you my date card is not so full these days. So, drink up and let us head out. Shall we?"

Brick looks over at Tj and shrugs his shoulders, "Well man, I guess I got to go. Big brother has spoken. Just remember who was winning here today, though." He takes a few more sips and finishes off his beer, as Stone downed him in one gulp.

"Are you okay to drive?" Stone inquired. "If not, we can take what you need and leave your car at the gym. I even promise not to tow you."

The guys did just that and headed to Stone's place in silence. Once home, they did not make it inside good before Stone got down to business.

"Listen bro, I will always have your back, no matter what. And you know I love Shae like a sister, a mean sister but a sister, nonetheless. You know you have a great thing with her. So, what gives? Is arguing over a fight that probably should not happen serious enough to cause permanent damage to your relationship?"

Walking over to the fridge, Brick opened it, looking deep inside for a beer. He found two, pulling one out for him and the other he handed to Stone.

"I've already told you and she both. That night, that fight, Ryker stole something from me. I am fighting to get that back. I lost the fight, but my dignity went out the door as well. No one seems to understand. I am the one who can barely sleep at night. When I do, I am fearful that I will sleep too hard. Or end up hurting my wife when I wake up in a fit." He shook his head. "Do you know I have hit her a few times already?" He could see the mortified look on Stone's face as he continued. "All she does is try to hold me and tell me it is going to be okay. She took each of the hits and not griped about it. Not once."

"She sounds like the amazing woman I know her to be. So, what is the problem?"

"She shouldn't have to console me after an episode or PTSD flare up. I'm the man," he said as he hit himself in the chest with a clenched fist repeatedly.

"Dude, no one, including your wife, is debating your manhood. That has never been in question. You need to put your ego aside because that is where I think the problem stems from. I mean, I could be wrong, but damn man; you are not the first to be knocked down and won't be the last. If you get in the ring, there is always a fifty—fifty chance that could happen. You know as well as I do, all it takes is one lucky hit and it can change the outcome of the fight. Are you willing to risk it again?"

"If you need to tell me something Stone, out with-it bro? You think I'm not ready?"

"I know you have been working hard. I have seen it. All I am trying to say is, don't let your foolish pride make you lose everything. Shae is resilient but sometimes bro she does not need to be. I think you should pull out of this one. There will be others."

"Others perhaps, but not this one. I love Shae with my life. But if I do not do this, I won't be any good for her, man."

"Then I guess there is nothing more to say about it. I'm behind you." Stone patted him on the back. "Why don't you get some sleep? You know where the spare bedroom is. There are towels in the shower. You will definitely need them judging by your not so fruity smell," Stone chuckled lightly.

Brick did a quick spin move to show off his skills, as he put Stone in one of his submission holds.

"Good one," Stone said right before he broke free.

The guys said their good nights going their separate ways. Stone had some film to look at, so that he could make sure Brick was as prepped as he could be.

Brick took his bags to the spare bedroom down the hall and on the left. Kicking his shoes off, he pulled his phone from his pocket. Disappointment followed, as he had no missed calls or text messages from Shae. As much of a man as he was, he was missing his woman. He missed her fussing, her kisses, and her voice. People often told her she sounded like the singer Pink. Brick played back his last few voicemails from her.

Babe, I just wanted to say I love you, but I guess you are already into your workout at the gym. I'll see you this evening. Love you.

Babe call me. Love you.

He played them back once more before putting his phone on the nightstand and going to get into the shower. The day's events had more than exhausted him, however, the water relaxed the tension he felt as it covered him. After his shower, he dried off and fell into the bed, where sleep came quickly for him.

Chapter Fourteen

SHAE

It had been two and a half weeks since she had seen her husband. This was not the life she wanted nor felt she could get used to. The two had been texting daily for about a week now thanks to Stone's intervening.

Shae's boss Cassandra had gone by the gym originally looking for Brick, but he was not there, so Stone sufficed. Cassandra was beyond over her brash demeanor. She begged him to do something. Shae had been in a funk. It was taking its toll on her writing and putting the others in the office at risk. Honestly, she'd had enough. She wanted her old Shae back. Stone promised to help, and his plan actually worked. Tonight, Shae and Brick were going on a dinner date.

Shae had picked a restaurant called Casablanca.

Their steaks were said to be quite amazing. She wanted tonight to be special. She had to put her feelings aside and be there for Brick.

Rodney interrupted her thoughts. Shae hadn't even noticed him entering the room.

"Did you change your mind? Please say you are going to write the piece for me. I know it is a big ask. I mean, it is your husband."

"Rodney, Rodney, Rodney. This fight, this rematch, is not something I am behind. With that being said, I cannot in good conscious write a piece on it. Especially if it turns out not in his favor. I respectfully decline you again and I hope that you can understand my position," she pleaded.

"I get it Shae, I do, but you can't blame a guy for trying to keep the lights on in this place," he smirked and winked at her.

"You are a piece of work, Rodney. Thanks for understanding," Shae looked down at her watch, shaking her head at where the time had gone. She still had to run a few errands before getting ready to meet Brick later.

❦

SHAE ARRIVED AT CASABLANCA A FEW MOMENTS after Brick. He was still at the front, giving the hostess his name for their table. He turned and caught a glimpse of her while her perfume penetrated his nostrils. Brick had always loved how Versace smelled on her. It was funny to him that the name of the perfume was the total opposite of his wife. She did not go for all the fancy name brands; she just went by what she liked. Brick made sure that she stayed stocked up on this fragrance.

"Hey."

"Hey."

They spoke in unison.

Brick reached his hand out to Shae. She grabbed it as he pulled her in for a hug.

Shae could tell he was missing her just as much as she did him. When his mouth failed to speak his feelings, his hugs and body language revealed it all to her. A part of her was glad, but the other side wanted him to keep his focus if he went through with the fight.

"Ma'am, Sir your table is ready. I am Misty and I will be your server. Right this way please," as she extended her hand to show the direction.

Brick placed his hand on Shae's lower back and guided her in the direction Misty was walking.

Shae would hate to admit it, but his touch was electrifying. Being around him after being apart gave her butterflies.

Brick held her chair out for her to sit. He was always such the gentleman. Just one of his qualities. Shae noticed that he was freshly shaven, with a haircut. She turned her eyes away as he caught her staring. Shae blushed while he simply smiled.

Misty brought them over some water and took their order. Within a few moments, she brought them salads, with promises that their food would be out soon.

Shae and Brick were both nervous, and they welcomed the food.

Reaching across the table for his hand, Shae broke the silence. “I am glad that you decided to join me for dinner tonight. It is really good to see you,” she squeezed his hand while talking. “The house hasn’t been the same. There are no clothes on the floor,” she smiled. As, did he?

Taking a deep breath, Brick responded, “Shae, listen. I love you and I have missed you terribly. I don’t want to fight with you, and I damn sure don’t want to lose you. This has been so hard. When I’m training with the bag, all I see is you and a disapproving look. In all my fights, the one common thing that was present was you. It kills me knowing you won’t be there this time.”

"Babe, I still have a few days. Who knows, I may

show up. Rodney asked me to do a piece on you. I refused."

"Shae, when can I come home? Why did you refuse the piece? Writing is your world, well, besides me."

"I didn't kick you out. You left, remember? I refused the piece because how would it look me trying to write a piece and your hurt? And before you say anything. I do believe in you and that you can win. But, what if?"

"I thought it was best. I still think it was the right thing. Things have been weird on my side, more so since the talk of this fight. I just wanted to make you proud of me. You used to love watching me in the ring, and that is the energy that I thrived on. Now I feel as if I have failed you in so many ways. Shae, I know you believe in me."

"You have not failed me. But no matter how much I say it, you must know it. So, I get it. I get why you have a need to do this, and I respect it."

Shae stood up and walked around the table to where Brick sat. She placed her hands on either side of his face and planted a passionate kiss before returning to her seat. Shae had her own way of driving him insane in zero seconds flat.

Just as she was sitting down, the waitress returned with their food. They ate with minimal conversation, only touching on how well it tasted or that the server forgot the cup of extra sauce Shae had requested. They laughed and joked about Casandra and her new friend. Brick said that he would have to tease her the next time he saw her.

After they finished off their meal, they left the restaurant, Brick walked her to her car.

"Do you want to come by the house tonight?" Shae asked coyly.

"I would love to, but when I come home, I want it to be for good. Tonight, is not for good. And just so you know, I did not want to leave, but I felt if I were going to go through with this, I had to. The fact that I am causing you to hurt daily because of my stubbornness would tear me apart. Trust me, being away is no walk in the park. I hate it." Brick confessed for the first time out loud.

He opened the car door as she slid into the driver's seat.

"I love you and I hope it goes the way you want and need it to."

Brick bends his head into the car to kiss her before shutting her door. He stood frozen in place as she drove off.

Sighing, he says to himself, "*I can't wait to go home. This is so much harder than I thought it would be.*" He walks to his car, debating whether he should go home or head back to Stone's. After a few moments of going back and forth with himself, he decides to see this through. He pulls off and heads in the direction of Stone's place.

THE NEXT FEW DAYS PASSED IN A BLUR FOR SHAE. The only thing that held her attention for a bit was that the next morning after her date with Brick, she had gotten sick. She attributed it to food poisoning and made a mental note to check the reviews to see if it happened to anyone else.

The dreaded fight night had arrived. Shae was still battling with herself to see if she would be attending. Her heart won that battle. She arrived after the fight had just begun. She heard the bell signifying the beginning of the round. Stone waved her over to their corner. She sat down quickly because she did not want to break Brick's concentration. She was in luck; he did not see her enter.

Shae had always loved watching him fight. Watching him move tonight almost felt like old times.

Ryker threw a combo of three punches, the third of which seemed to have stunned Brick a bit as it landed on his nose. Brick recovered and countered with a combo of his own that ended with a kick. Shae saw the brief smile that crept to his face. They danced around in the middle of the ring for another minute or two before the bell sounded.

Stone goes over and talks to Brick.

"You okay, buddy? Guess who showed up for you?"

Brick turned and caught sight of his wife, sitting behind him, wearing his colors of purple and gold. She smiled, and he smiled back. Shae mouthed the words, "I love you." Brick responded with, "I know and thank you."

After the bell rung to start round two, Stone made his way back to where Shae was sitting.

"Is he okay?" Shae asked.

"He is even better now that you are here. No matter what happens, he needed you here in his corner. Believe it or not, he is doing well for someone who was where he was a while ago."

Shae never took her eyes off the fight. Brick threw a punch to Ryker's gut, then another jab that did not connect. Ryker threw a few left right combos before striking Brick with his left foot across the shin. Brick looked down briefly and Ryker hit him with a right jab to the side of his left temple. They continued to exchange punches into the second round. Shae was on the edge of her seat when the bell rung.

Shae sat and watched as Stone went again to check on his guy before returning to her side. The final round started off routinely. Neither of the fighters were super aggressive. Shae could see that Ryker had something to prove. Brick still was fighting a good fight, even not at 100%, so his critics were right to feel like he got lucky.

Ryker was throwing a few jabs to Brick's left temple. Shae stood to her feet as another punch landed. Brick staggered back, losing his footing and fell to the mat after trying to catch hold of the rope. He hit his face hard when he went down. The referee stood there for a moment, dazed, as Ryker kept shouting for him to call it. Brick got up on his knees slowly at first and within a few more seconds, he was on his feet. Ryker did not like this at all. He walks over and headbutts Brick twice before the referee could stop it. Brick fell to the mat with a loud thud. Stone climbed inside the ring, shouting at Ryker.

"What gives? You are a punk. You want to fight, then fight me," he said as he knelt down over Brick. The fighter in him was trying to get up until he caught sight of the horror that filled Shae's eyes. He lay there. He refused to get up. He knew she was losing it. Nothing was worth that.

Shae felt as if she had been glued to her spot. As much as she wanted to go to him, Stone motioned for her to not. Her eyes filled with tears, and she could not keep them from falling.

Ding.......Ding...... the match was called after they made sure Brick was okay. The officials disqualified Ryker.

Chapter Fifteen

BRICK

"Are you okay? How many fingers do I have up," Stone continued without waiting for an answer. "We are about to put you on a stretcher, okay?"

"Wait.....wait a minute. I'm okay," he said as he rolled over and looked for his wife. "Tell Shae that I am okay. Did you see me, Stone? I hung in there, but he caught me slipping."

"Yeah bro, you did it."

Brick's eyelids blinked repeatedly before his eyes finally closed. The paramedics were there, putting him on to a flatbed, and then to the gurney as they rushed him out of the arena.

Stone went and got Shae and the two of them followed the ambulance to St. Christian's Hospital. Once they arrived, they were shown where Brick had been taken.

Shae was pacing back and forth as Stone tried to talk to her.

"He is going to be okay Shae. I told you he trained really hard for this one."

"The last time he fought, and we ended up in a place like this, it wasn't okay. I'm sorry if I can't get on board that he is good until I see him and or the doctors tell me he is okay," she spoke through clenched teeth.

BRICK TRIED TO OPEN HIS EYES WHEN HE HEARD the Doctor asking him, but it was so hard. His eyelids fluttered and finally opened.

"Hi Brick, my name is Dr. Mitch. Looks like you took a beating."

Brick let out a groan as the doctor touched his abdomen. Dr. Mitch kept doing his examination, apologizing as he hit tender spots. He checked his eyes to ensure he could follow his fingers as he moved them in different directions. Brick squeezed the Dr's fingers when asked to do so.

"I know that wasn't the most pleasant exam, but I do thank you for your patience. Without doing an MRI, and because I know you are a fighter, I can tell you definitively that you have a mild concussion. The great news is that you are going to be just fine," he paused before continuing. "You know there is a lady out there who says she is your wife; she looks kind of worried. What do you think? Can I bring her back before she gets her bodyguard to attack my staff when they are walking by?"

Brick nodded yes as a tear rolled down his cheek. The doctor reaches for the call button and presses it. Nurse Jill replied. He requested that she send in the lady with the bodyguard. Nurse Jill said, of course, and laughed. Within a few moments the door to the room opened and Shae entered, while Stone stayed outside the door.

Shae walked to Brick's bedside and grabbed his hand. He squeezed hers.

"Babe, I told you I was going to be okay. This old dog still has some fight in him."

"You did good, babe. I am so proud of you," Shae said before the dr interrupted.

"Your husband is going to be just fine. A few contusions, bruises, and a mild concussion, but nothing is broken. You guys can go home in the morning. I ordered an MRI just to be sure I missed nothing."

Shae bent down and kissed Brick full on the lips. "I love you."

"Thank you, Dr.,"

"Shae babe, I don't want to ever lose you. Sometimes I lose sight of the fact that you have been in my corner, holding me down for so long. I think I take you for granted and I don't mean to. I love you. Please never leave me."

Shae bent down to whisper in his ear, "I would not think of it. Besides, you are going to be a daddy."

Brick eyes filled with tears again. "How!"

"Really?"

"Are you sure?"

"Yes"

"Does anyone know?

"Just you."

"Thank you, Babe."

THE END

Although DaKiara is still considered new to the publishing world, she has hit the ground running full speed ahead. In her first year, she independently published her first work. Soon after, she decided to form Mind Flow Publishing LLC, a small publishing house, to work with other authors. DaKiara has recently earned a spot on the Amazon International Bestsellers List. She has become a frequent flyer on the Amazon US Bestsellers List. Each time for her feels as if it is the first all over again. Her works are spread across genres such as Poetry, Inspirational, Urban Fiction, Paranormal, Contemporary Romance, Suspense & Thriller, and Christian Fiction.

In addition to having books available in paperback, and eBook formats, DaKiara has an ever-growing catalog on Amazon's newest platform, Vella. Some of those titles are Inn Too Deep, Split Decision, and Finding Kate. These have been some of her more popular projects. All are completed and will be moving to eBook and paperback in 2023.

DaKiara's love for writing started when she was

about twelve, writing poetry and writing speeches for various oratorical contests. Inspiration for her craft is pulled from her own life experiences, as well as others. She has been featured on several podcasts, as well as Up and Coming Authors Newsletters. When she is not writing, she loves to design shadowboxes and create personalized greeting cards.

Thank You for Reading....

ALSO BY DAKIARA

Also By DaKiara

The Mary B Chronicles

For Her Love

Standalone Short Stories

Charisma's Homecoming

Dreams Do Come True

A Chance at Love

Young Adult

Royalty

Occult & Horror

To Be Chosen

Inspirational

Journey to Living

Poetry

Mental Interlude

Simple Complexity

Spoken from the Heart

Falling in Love with Poetry

UPCOMING PROJECTS BY DAKIARA

- Secrets Uncovered Series
- Sleepless Nights (1)
- Dark Truths (2)
- Redeeming Justice (3)
- Sins of the Past (4)
- Balance of Power (5)
- For Her Love 2
- Dragon Slayer
- The Birthday Wish
- Inn Too Deep
- Sophie's Pack
- Split Decision
- Finding Kate

All titles will be available on Vella. All titles will be in eBook and paperback formats once completed.

www.ingramcontent.com/pod-product-compliance
Lightning Source LLC
La Vergne TN
LVHW051006080826
845145LV00009B/2490

* 9 7 8 1 9 5 1 2 7 1 2 2 0 *